DEAR SANTASAURUS

BOYDS MILLS PRESS

AN IMPRINT OF HIGHLIGHTS

Honesdale, Pennsylvania

Boyds Mills Press
An Imprint of Highlights
815 Church Street
Honesdale, Pennsylvania 18431
boydsmillspress.com
Printed in China

ISBN: 978-1-59078-876-9
Library of Congress Control Number: 2013931087

First edition

10 9 8 7 6 5 4 3 2 1

To Cora, Lily, & Henry
—SM

To my mom
—JK

January 1

Dear Santasaurus,

  Thank you. Thank you! THANK YOU!!! I love my remote-control flying pterodactyl. One wing broke, so it doesn't fly anymore. But that's OK, because I lost the remote.

  Have a Happy New Year. I promise to stay on the Nice List all year.

                              Your friend,
                              Ernest B. Spinosaurus

February 14

Dear Santasaurus,

Happy Valentine's Day. I had to sign 19 cards, one for each dinosaur in my class. I had an extra and thought of you. Hope this keeps me on the Nice List.

Gotta go. My best friend, Ty, dared me to check out the volcano behind his house. A little ash and smoke don't scare me.

Your friend,
Ernest B. Spinosaurus

P.S. I didn't think Mom would be that afraid of a fake spider in her box of chocolates.

March 19

Dear Santasaurus,

    Have you started the Naughty List yet? My sister, Amber, really needs to be on it. It was *her* idea for me to sneak behind Granny and yell, "Meteor shower!" Not mine.

    I've been thinking about my Christmas list. I want a scooter. No need to thank me for putting in my order early. That's what nice dinos do.

                    Your friend,
                    Ernest B. Spinosaurus

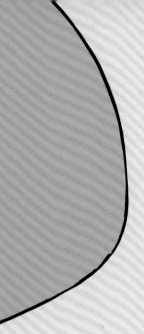

April 1

Dear Santasaurus,

    For Christmas, I want rainbow underwear with white polka dots. Seven hundred pairs of underwear. And Ty wants a thousand pairs of socks. That's it. No toys. No scooter.

               Your friend,
               Ernest B. Spinosaurus

PS: Just kidding. APRIL FOOL'S DAY! Ha ha ha.

April 2

Dear Santasaurus,

Yesterday's letter was a joke. You knew that, right? I do NOT want seven hundred pairs of underwear for Christmas. I don't want any underwear. I want the Jurassic Turbo Scooter X9.

Please, please, please do not bring me any underwear.

Your friend,
Ernest B. Spinosaurus

PS: Ty doesn't want socks, either.

May 13

Dear Santasaurus,

    Today, I scored two soccer goals (one for my team, one for the other team). I ate all my dinner (except for what dropped on the floor). I even helped Amber take her first steps. So let's forget about yesterday's mess with the glitter glue, paint, and Dad's toothbrush. Besides, Mom sure did like the Mother's Day card I made with my own claws.

    I've been thinking more about my Christmas list. I want the *Sea Serpent Blue* Jurassic Turbo Scooter X9. I also want a Raging Raptor action figure.

    Please.

Your friend,
Ernest B. Spinosaurus

June 14

Dear Santasaurus,

Hooray! I got a Raging Raptor for my birthday, so you can cross it off my list. I'm thinking of something else. Tar Pit Goo. You can stretch it, stick it, and paint with it. It's awesome. And maybe you could get some for Ty, too. I accidentally ate his.

Your friend,
Ernest B. Spinosaurus

PS: Did you know the Jurassic Turbo Scooter X9 has a working headlight?

July 20

Dear Santasaurus,

Having a great time at the beach. The lifeguard only had to tell me four times to stop scaring the little dinosaurs with my fin. I've learned my lesson. But maybe you already knew that?

Your friend,

Ernest B. Spinosaurus

August 8

Dear Santasaurus,

I am sooo on the Nice List. I've learned about being helpful at scout camp. If you want, I can tie the string of your sack into an awesome knot. I've been practicing on Amber's tail.

I definitely deserve the *Fungus Green* Jurassic Turbo Scooter X9 WITH the racing fin.

Your friend,
Ernest B. Spinosaurus

September 26

Dear Santasaurus,

I've enclosed my school picture. Dad didn't like my choice of shirt (or the fake frill and mustache). I said you should decide. Is it naughty or nice? Nice, right?

Ty saved his allowance to buy a Jurassic Turbo Scooter X9. It's *River Rage Purple* and has the headlight, the racing fin, and a hand brake. It's cool, but a *Cosmic Orange* scooter would be even better since it has a secret compartment.

Your friend,
Ernest B. Spinosaurus

October 31

Dear Santasaurus,

Yes, I added a fourth horn to Mr. Triceratops's jack-o'-lanterns. But he was handing out leaves and branches instead of candy. If I get a Jurassic Turbo Scooter X9 for Christmas I promise to never prank anyone again.

Your friend,
Ernest B. Spinosaurus

November 9

Dear Santasaurus,
    This is it. My final Christmas list. I wanted to carve it in stone, but Dad said I couldn't mail a stone.
    1. A *Moonless Night Black* Jurassic Turbo Scooter X9 with the matching water bottle
    2. Tar Pit Goo
    3. A Rock Tumbler

Your friend,
Ernest B. Spinosaurus

PS: And I'm really, really sorry about using Amber's art project as a napkin. That was a big oops on my part.

November 26

Dear Santasaurus,

Mom says Thanksgiving is a time when we should stop asking for stuff (like a *Stardust Silver* Jurassic Turbo Scooter X9 with a rearview mirror) and give thanks for what we have. I am a thankful dinosaur.

I'm thankful for my toys and the glue needed to fix them.
I'm thankful that I have only one sister.
I'm thankful for Ty and that I'm bigger than he is.
I'm thankful that I'll be riding a new Jurassic Turbo Scooter X9 in a month (hint, hint).

Your friend,
Ernest B. Spinosaurus

December 5

Dear Santasaurus,

By my count, I have a whopping 257 nice acts and only 256 naughty acts. I'm sending you my charts.

Guess what?! Did you know there is now a Jurassic Turbo Scooter X10? I want the *Lightning White* model that has the knobby claw grips.

Your friend,

Ernest B. Spinosaurus

December 6

Dear Santasaurus,

   I took a bath without being told and even used water. That definitely makes up for putting my muddy socks in the refrigerator. Sorry. Ty told me that's how fossils are made.

Your friend,
Ernest B. Spinosaurus

December 24

Dear Santasaurus,

Welcome to our house. Mom and I baked the cookies and Amber added the sprinkles.

Don't forget, I want the *Lava Red* Jurassic Turbo Scooter X10 with the working headlight, the racing fin, the hand brake, the secret compartment, the matching water bottle, the rearview mirror, the knobby claw grips, and the siren. We both really like red. And I think Amber wants a tricycle. Probably pink.

Thank you!

Your friend,
Ernest B. Spinosaurus

January 1

Dear Santasaurus,

Thank you. Thank you! THANK YOU!!! I love my scooter. It's exactly what I wanted. The handlebars got bent and the brakes are crushed, but that's OK, because it still flies going downhill.

Amber really likes her tricycle. The bell is her favorite part.

Have a Happy New Year. I promise to stay on the Nice List all year.

Your friend,

Ernest B. Spinosaurus

PS: Have you seen the new Yamawow Deluxe drum set with cymbals???

It rocks!